THE STORY OF
A BOLD TIN SOLDIER

LAURA LEE HOPE

THE STORY OF A BOLD TIN SOLDIER

CHAPTER I

A MAKE-BELIEVE FIGHT

"Attention!"

That was the word of command heard in the toy section of a large department store one night, after all the customers and clerks had gone home.

"Attention!"

"Dear me, what is going on?" asked a Calico Clown, as he looked around the corner of a pile of gaily colored building blocks.

"Has the Sawdust Doll come back to see us?" inquired a Candy Rabbit.

"That would be good news, if it were true," said a Jumping Jack.

"But it isn't true," announced a Monkey on a Stick, as he climbed up to the top of his perch and looked over the top of a Noah's Ark. "I don't see the Sawdust Doll anywhere, nor the White Rocking Horse, nor the Lamb on Wheels. It isn't any of our former friends who have come back to visit us."

"Who is it, then?" asked the Calico Clown, reaching up to get hold of a long string, for he thought perhaps he could turn somersaults like the Monkey on a Stick or the Jumping Jack.

"Attention, Soldiers!" suddenly called again the first voice that had spoken. "Ready, now! Attention!"

"Oh, it's the Bold Tin Soldier!" said the Jack in the Box, who was the Jumping Jack's cousin. "What's the matter down there in your barracks, my Bold Tin Soldier?" went on the Box-Jack, as he was sometimes called for short.

"I want my men to get ready to march," answered the Bold Tin Soldier. "We are going to have a fancy drill to amuse you, my friends. Would you like to see me march my men around the counter?"

"Very much, indeed," answered the Candy Rabbit. "It is night now, and there are no human eyes to see what we do. So we toys may come to life and move about and make believe we are real as much as we please. We haven't had very much fun since the jolly sailor came and carried away the Lamb on Wheels."

"Has any one heard anything from her since she left us?" asked the Calico Clown.

"Oh, yes, the Lamb has a lovely home with a little girl named Mirabell," answered the Jack in the Box. "And Mirabell has a brother named Arnold, and those two children live next door to Dorothy, who has our dear friend the Sawdust Doll."

"Really?" asked the Jumping Jack.

"Really and truly," added the Box-Jack. "And Dorothy's brother, whose name is Dick, owns the White Rocking Horse who used to be here with us."

"Why, that is quite remarkable," said the Monkey on a Stick. "I hope we all get homes with such nice children when we are sold and taken away."

"You may well say that," came from the Bold Tin Soldier. "Some children are not as kind to their toys as they might be. But now, if you want to see me and my men march around in fancy drill, please take your places and keep out of the way."

"Yes, indeed, we must keep out of the way," said the Candy Rabbit. "I don't want to get pricked with a soldier's bayonet or tickled with the Captain's sword."

"And be sure to keep well back from the edge of the counter," went on the Bold Tin Soldier. "I don't want any of you falling off when the guns are fired."

"Oh dear me! has any one a bit of cotton?" asked a Rag Doll, who sat next to a picture book.

"Cotton? Why do you want cotton?" asked the Calico Clown.

"Didn't you hear what the Bold Tin Soldier said?" asked the Rag Doll. "He spoke about guns going to be shot off, and I can't bear loud noises. If I can find some cotton I am going to stuff it into my ears so I won't be made deaf."

The Box-Jack and the Jumping Jack stood side by side as cousins ought; the Candy Rabbit found a place near the Noah's Ark; the Monkey on a Stick found a place as near the parade grounds as the Bold Captain would let him come; and the Calico Clown moved over close to the Rag Doll.

"If the guns should, by accident, shoot too loudly," said the Clown. "I will hold my hands over your ears, Miss Rag Doll."

"That is very kind of you," she answered with a smile. "But please do not bang your cymbals, as they make almost as much noise as the soldiers' guns."

"I'll be careful," promised the Calico Clown, who wore a gay suit of many colors, one leg being red and the other yellow, while his shirt was spotted, speckled and striped. On the end of each arm was a round disk of brass.

These were called "cymbals," and when any one pressed on the Clown's chest he moved his arms and banged his cymbals together with a clanging sound.

"Attention!" called the Bold Tin Soldier again, and at this word of command the other Tin Soldiers in the box with their Captain stood up and began to move into line, each one carrying his gun over his shoulder.

As I have told you in my other books, the toys could pretend to come to life and move about after dark, when no one was in the store to see them. The toys could also move about by themselves in the day time, if no human eyes watched them. But as there was nearly always some one–either clerk or customer–in the store during the day, the toys seldom had a chance to do as they pleased during daylight hours. So most of their fun took place after dark, as was happening now.

"Attention!" once more called the Captain. "Get ready, my brave men! Forward–March!"

And then while some of the Soldiers who had fifes, drums, trumpets and horns played a lively tune, the others, led by their Captain, marched along. They went down the toy counter and paraded past the place where the Candy Rabbit sat watching them. Straight and stiff marched the Tin Soldiers, the music of the tin band becoming more and more lively.

"Left, wheel!" called the Captain, and the Tin Soldiers turned to the left.

"Right, wheel!" shouted the Captain, and the Tin Soldiers turned to the right.

Then they marched around in a circle, and they marched in a square, and they marched in a triangle, and in all sorts of fancy figures. They swung around the Rag Doll, and the Captain waved his shiny sword so fast that the Calico Clown cried:

"Oh, it is so dazzling bright that it hurts my eyes!"

And then the Bold Tin Soldier Captain led his men up a hill made of a pile of building blocks.

"Oh, I hope they do not fall off!" said the Rag Doll.

"No, they won't fall," answered the Candy Rabbit. "I guess the Captain knows what he is doing."

Straight up the building-block hill the Bold Tin Soldier led his men, and when they reached the top he cried:

"Jump!"

"Oh mercy me!" screamed the Rag Doll, "they'll all be killed!"

And those Tin Soldiers, who, like other soldiers, must always obey their officers, jumped right off the top of the building-block hill.

But they were not killed, nor was one of them hurt, I am glad to say. For at the bottom of the pile of blocks was a rubber football, and the Soldiers landed on this, bounced up and down, and then gently landed on the counter. The Captain knew the football was there, or he would not have told his men to jump.

"My, that was a fine drill!" said the Rag Doll. "How exciting!"

"Hush! They are going to do something else," said the Monkey on a Stick.

And it did seem so, for part of the Soldiers, shouldering their guns, marched to one end of the toy counter, and the others, with their Captain at their head, remained near the pile of blocks.

"Are you ready?" asked the Captain of a Sergeant who had charge of the second half of the tin soldiers.

"All ready, sir!" was the answer.

"Load! Aim! Fire!" suddenly cried the Captain.

"Oh, they are going to shoot! Oh, it's going to be war! There is going to be a battle!" cried the Rag Doll.

"Nonsense! It is only going to be a make-believe battle!" said the Calico Clown. "Our Captain told me about it. It is to be a sham battle to amuse us. See, they are aiming their guns at one another!"

And as he spoke the Rag Doll looked and saw the two companies of Tin Soldiers ready to take part in a battle.

"Oh, hold me! Hold me!" whispered the Rag Doll to the Calico Clown. "I know I am going to faint!"

CHAPTER II

SAVING THE CLOWN

"Ready! Take aim! Fire!" cried the Bold Tin Soldier Captain.

"Bang! Bang!" cracked the tin guns, some in the hands of one "army" and some shot off by the other "army." The Soldiers had divided themselves into two "armies," to give a make-believe fight to amuse the other toys.

"Crack! Crack! Bang! Bang!" rattled the tin guns.

But the guns were so small and there was such a little bit of the make-believe powder in each one that the noise they made would not have broken an egg, to say nothing of hurting the ears of a Rag Doll.

"Are you going to faint?" asked the Calico Clown of the Doll. He stood with his arms stretched out, ready to catch her in case she did.

"No! No, I don't believe I shall faint!" she answered. "Ha! Ha! Ha!" she suddenly laughed.

"What is so funny?" asked the Calico Clown. "I didn't tell a joke or ask a riddle, did I?" For that is what he sometimes did to make the toys in the department store laugh.

"No, you didn't do anything," answered the Rag Doll. "It is just that you look so funny, standing there ready to catch me with those brass things on your hands. Ha! Ha!"

"Those are my cymbals," said the Clown. "I can't let go of them. They are fastened on. Sometimes I get tired of them, but I cannot get rid of them."

"I know it, and it was too bad of me to laugh at you," answered the Rag Doll. "I did not mean to make fun of you, and it was very kind on your part, to be ready to catch me if I fainted. But you did look so funny!"

The Bold Tin Soldiers were doing their best to make some entertainment for the other toys.

"Ready! Aim! Fire!" cried the Captain to his men, again and again.

"Ready! Aim! Fire!" shouted the Sergeant to his men, for he had been given command of half the toy Soldiers for this sham fight.

The guns popped, the Soldiers rushed back and forth on the toy counter. Some pretended to be hit and fell down as natural as anything.

But at last the Bold Tin Soldier Captain and his men seemed to be winning. Most of the Captain's Soldiers were up on their feet, while quite a number of the Sergeant's men had fallen over.

"Surrender! Surrender! Give up!" shouted the Captain, as he rushed with his men toward the Sergeant and his men. "Surrender! Hoist the white flag!"

"All right, it is hoisted!" answered the Sergeant, and he tied his handkerchief on the end of his gun, where the stickery thing, called a bayonet, was fastened. "We surrender!" said the Sergeant.

"All right! Stop firing!" called the Captain to his men. "We have captured the enemy and the battle is over."

"I'm so glad it was only a make-believe one, and no one was hurt," sighed the Rag Doll.

"It was very jolly, all right," said the Candy Rabbit. "This is the first make-believe fight I ever saw. Are you going to have another, Captain?"

"Not to-night," was the reply. "My men are tired, but we are glad if you toys enjoyed our efforts."

"We certainly did," declared the Monkey on a Stick. "I wish I had joined the army instead of going through life on a stick, climbing to the top and climbing down again," he added, with a sigh.

"Oh, well, we cannot all be soldiers," said the Jack in the Box.

"No, indeed," agreed the Candy Rabbit. "If I had a gun I should not know what to do with it. It is only brave men, like our Bold Captain and his men, who know how to use swords and guns," he concluded.

"Thank you," said the Captain, waving his shiny sword. "We are glad you liked our drill and make-believe fight. Form in line, ready to go back to your box, my men," he went on.

Led by the Sergeant, under whom some of them had fought in the pretended battle, the Tin Soldiers formed in line, ready to march back to the box in which they were kept on the toy counter.

"I wonder what will happen to-day," remarked the Calico Clown, as he looked out through a distant window. "It will soon be morning," he went on. "I can see the sun beginning to redden the sky in the east. I wonder if any of us will be sold and taken away."

"It might happen," said the Bold Tin Soldier. "If I have to go I hope my men may come with me."

"Oh, of course they'll go with you," said the Rag Doll. "Who ever heard of a Soldier Captain without some men under him? You will all go together, for you belong in the same box."

"I'm sure I hope so," went on the Captain. "I suppose I shall be bought and given to some boy. Girls, as a rule, don't care very much for soldiers. They would rather have a Sawdust Doll or a Lamb on Wheels. And if I am given to some boy, I hope he will be like the boys we have heard about–Dick, the brother of Dorothy, and Arnold, the brother of Mirabell."

"Yes, they are nice boys, from what I have heard," said the Calico Clown. "Well, it will soon be bright daylight, and then we shall see what happens," he added.

"Yes, we'll see," said the Captain. Then, turning to his men, he commanded:

"Ready–March."

Off to their box marched the Tin Soldiers led by the Sergeant, who was next in command to the Captain. There ought to have been a First and Second Lieutenant, but the man who made the tin toys had forgotten them.

So the Sergeant led the Tin Soldiers back to their box after the make-believe battle. And, like good and proper soldiers, they stood themselves in straight rows. No standing around in a crowd, or lying down in hammocks, or stretching out under trees for these Tin Soldiers!

No, indeed! They stood up as straight and stiff as their own guns!

"Did you like our drill and sham battle?" asked the Bold Tin Soldier Captain of the Rag Doll, strolling over to speak to her before going back to join his men.

"Very much, indeed," she answered. "At first I thought I might faint when the guns shot off, but they were fired so gently that I did not, and the Calico Clown did not have to catch me in his arms."

"I don't let my Soldiers use too much powder in their guns," answered the Captain. "It is a sort of tooth powder we use in these make-believe fights, and then no one is hurt."

"It will be lonesome if you go away from us," said the Rag Doll, with a sigh, as she looked at the Bold Tin Soldier.

"Thank you for being so kind as to say that," said the Bold Tin Soldier. "But I have no notion of going away until I have to."

However, he little knew what was going to happen nor that he was to be taken away much sooner than he expected.

"I had better be getting over to the box with my Soldiers, I think," said the Captain, as he thrust his shiny sword back into the scabbard at his side. "Our fun for to-night is over."

"No, not quite yet," said the Calico Clown. "The sun has not yet risen, and it will be ten minutes before the watchman comes in to turn out the lights and get the store ready for the day's trade."

"But what can be done in ten minutes?" asked the Rag Doll.

"I can do a funny trick for you," said the Clown. "I have not yet done my share towards the night's fun, so I will do my trick now."

"Are you going to tell a joke or ask a riddle?" inquired the Candy Rabbit. "If you are, I wish you'd tell that one about what makes more noise than a pig under a gate."

"No, I am going to do a funny trick. Do you see that string there!" he asked the other toys, pointing upward.

"Do you mean the one hanging near the gas jet?" asked the Box Jack.

"Yes," answered the Clown. "Well, I am going to climb that string and hang by my toes."

He quickly walked over to a long string that hung down from the ceiling. At Christmas time it had held some wreaths of holly, but now nothing was fast to it.

"Up I go!" cried the Clown.

It was hard work for him to climb the string with the cymbals fast on the ends of his arms, but he managed to get up nearly as high as the flaming gas jet which lighted the store at night, so the watchman could see his way around.

"That's high enough–don't go up any farther!" cried the Bold Tin Soldier.

"Yes, I am high enough now," said the Clown. "Watch me hang by my toes!"

He began turning over as he clung to the string, and, as he did so, he began to sway to and fro, like the pendulum of a clock.

"Look out! Look out for the blazing gas light! You'll be burned!" suddenly called the Rag Doll.

And as she spoke, the Clown on the dangling string came too near the gas flame. His baggy trousers, one leg red and the other yellow, began to smoke.

"Oh, the Calico Clown is burning! He will catch fire!" cried the Candy Rabbit. "Will no one save him?"

"Yes, I'll save the Calico Clown!" cried the Bold Tin Soldier, and he drew his shining sword. "I will save him!"

CHAPTER III

BOUGHT BY A BOY

The toys were very much excited when they saw the Calico Clown beginning to burn, because he had swung too near the gas jet.

"Oh, I can't bear to look at him!" cried the Rag Doll, covering her eyes with her hands.

"He'll be all right! The Bold Tin Soldier is going to save him," said the Monkey on a Stick.

"But how can he?" asked the Jumping Jack. "How can the Captain get up there and save our Clown? The string will not hold two!"

And, indeed, the Bold Tin Soldier himself was beginning to wonder how he could save his toy friend. He could not scramble up the string, as the Clown had done, and, if he did, the Bold Captain might catch fire himself.

Of course a tin soldier will not burn as quickly as a Clown with a suit of cloth, but the gas flame was very hot and dangerous.

"Come down! Come down!" cried the Rag Doll. "Come down, Mr. Calico Clown!"

And that, you would have thought, would have been the easiest way for the comical chap to save himself–just to slide down the string to the counter. But something had happened.

"I can't get down!" the Clown exclaimed. "The string is twisted around my leg and caught on one of my cymbals! I can't get loose to come down!" And that is what had happened.

"But still I will save him!" cried the Bold Tin Soldier. He looked around the toy counter and saw a sofa cushion that belonged to a large doll's parlor set. "Quick!" shouted the Captain. "Put that cushion right under the Clown who is dangling by the string. Then when he falls he will not hurt himself. Over with the cushion!"

"But he can't fall!" said the Jack in the Box. "He's all tangled up in the string. He can't get loose!"

"I'll get him loose!" declared the Captain. "Some of you shove that soft cushion over under our Clown!"

The two Jacks, the Candy Rabbit and the Monkey on a Stick pulled and hauled until the cushion was just where the Clown would land if he let go of the string and fell. But he was still tangled in the string, and every time he swung, like the pendulum of the clock, he came close to the burning gas jet. And each time he did this his red and yellow trousers were scorched.

"Oh, will no one save me?" cried the Clown.

"Yes, I will!" shouted the Bold Tin Soldier. "I am going to cut the string with my sword. Then you will fall down, but you will not be hurt because you will fall on the sofa cushion. I'll cut the string with my shiny tin sword, and then you won't be burned."

Near the string which dangled from the ceiling was a Japanese Juggler with a long ladder, which he could climb, balancing a ball on the end of his nose. Just now the Juggler was resting at the foot of the ladder that stood upright. The Juggler did not speak English very well, and that is why he did not understand all that was going on. He had not said a word since the Clown had climbed the string and had swung too near the blazing gas jet.

"Will you allow me to use your ladder, Mr. Japanese Juggler?" called the Bold Tin Soldier to the chap with the ball on the end of his nose.

"Without waiting for an answer, which he hardly expected, the Captain sprang up the ladder, holding his sword ready. In an instant he stood near the swaying, swinging Clown who waved to and fro on the string.

"Swish! Swash!"

That was the shiny tin sword sweeping through the air. The string was sliced in two pieces.

The Clown was cut loose, and down he fell on the soft sofa cushion, not being hurt at all. He was saved from burning.

"Hurray! Hurray for our brave Captain!" cried all the toys, clapping their hands, and the China Cat clapped his paws, which were just the same as hands.

"Are you all right?" asked the Bold Tin Soldier after he had climbed down the ladder and hurried over to where the Clown was getting up off the sofa cushion.

"Yes, thank you! I am all right," was the answer. "I should not have tried to swing by that string so near the burning gas. But I did not think. Now, oh dear! Look at my trousers!"

Well might the clown say that, for his fine yellow and red trousers were scorched and burned. It was lucky the Clown himself was not burned, but it was too bad his suit was spoiled.

"Oh dear me! no one will ever buy me now," said the Clown sadly, looking at his legs. "I am damaged! I'll be thrown into the waste-paper basket!"

"Perhaps I could make you a new suit," said the Rag Doll. "I can sew a little, and if I had some cloth I might at least put a patch over the burned places if I shouldn't have time for a whole suit."

"Thank you," answered the Clown. "But I would never look the same. And thank you, Captain, for cutting me down before I was burned," he went on to the Bold Tin Soldier. "It was very brave of you."

"Oh, it was nothing," the Captain modestly said. "We soldiers are here to do just such things as that."

"Hush!" suddenly called the Monkey on a Stick. "Here come the clerks. The store is going to open!"

And so all the toys had to be quiet and go back to their places. They could not make believe be alive until night should come again.

One by one the girl clerks took their places behind the toy counters near the shelves on which the different playthings were stored. One girl picked up the Calico Clown.

"Well, I do declare!" exclaimed this girl. "Look at my fancy Clown, will you, Mabel?"

"What's the matter with him, Sallie?" asked the clerk whose name was Mabel.

"Why, his red and yellow pants are scorched," answered Sallie. "I wonder what happened to him. Some customer who was smoking must have dropped a match or some hot cigar ashes on him. I must tell the manager about this. I can't sell a damaged toy like that."

"No, you can't," agreed Mabel, after she had looked at the poor Calico Clown.

"Oh, but I know what we can do!" the girl clerk suddenly exclaimed. "What?" asked Sallie.

And "what?" wondered the Clown.

"We can make him a new pair of trousers," was the answer. "Up in my locker I have some pieces of silk I had left over when I dressed my little sister's doll for Christmas. I'll get my needle and thread and the pieces of silk, and this noon, at lunch hour, we'll make a new suit for the Clown. Then he won't be damaged, and you can sell him."

"Oh, that will be fine!" cried the other girl, and the Clown, hearing this, felt much better.

By this time customers were coming into the store to buy toys and other things, and the toy counters and shelves were busy places. The Bold Tin Soldier had gone back to his box with his men, and there he and they stood, straight and stiff as ramrods, waiting for what might happen to them.

All the toys wished to talk about the brave rescue of the Calico Clown by the Captain, but of course they had to keep still.

"But we can talk about it to-night," thought the Candy Rabbit to himself. "We'll have a grand time when the store is once more closed. But I hope the Clown does no more of his tricks. The next time his jacket might burn, as well as his trousers."

The girl who had promised to make a new pair of gay silk trousers for the Clown was kept very busy that morning waiting on customers. She had just sold a little Celluloid Doll to a small girl when a boy and a man came walking past the counter behind which she stood.

"There's what I want, right over there!" said the boy, pointing.

"What is it?" asked the man, who seemed to be his father.

"That set of soldiers," went on the boy. "I want that Bold Tin Soldier Captain, who carries a sword, and I would like a set of his tin men. Then Dick and I can play war and battle and have lots of fun."

"I'm afraid that set of toy soldiers will cost too much," replied the man. "You know I said you could have a toy, but not one that is too expensive."

"Well, let's ask how much the tin soldiers cost," suggested the boy.

"That set costs two dollars," answered the girl behind the counter.

"And I said you could have only a dollar, Arnold," said the man.

"I have a dollar of my own pocket money that I have been saving," said the boy. "If I put that with your dollar I'll have two! Then couldn't I get the Captain and his men?"

"Yes, I suppose you could," answered the man slowly.

"Then I'm going to buy them!" exclaimed the boy. "Hurray! I'm going to have a Bold Tin Soldier and his men."

"Well, now I suppose my adventures will begin," thought the Captain, for he heard all that was said. "Like the Sawdust Doll, the White Rocking Horse, and the Lamb on Wheels, I am to be sold and taken away. Yes, now my adventures will begin!"

The girl clerk went to get a piece of wrapping paper in which to do up the box of soldiers. The boy and his father stepped aside for a moment to look at some other toys. As they were out of sight of the counter for a few seconds, and as no one was watching, the Calico Clown had a chance to whisper to the Captain.

"So you are going away from us?" asked the Clown.

"Yes," answered the Captain. "But I am sorry I shall not see the new trousers the girl is going to make for you. I would like to see them."

"Perhaps you may come back and visit us," suggested the Candy Rabbit.

"Perhaps," agreed the Captain, and then he had to stop talking for the boy and his father came back.

CHAPTER IV

A BEAN BATTLE

"Well, Arnold, do you think you will like your Bold Tin Soldier and his men?" asked the boy's father.

"Oh, yes, Daddy! I'm sure I shall!" was the answer. "I'll take them over to Dick's house, and we'll have a make-believe battle on the floor in the playroom."

"That is strange," thought the tin Captain, as the girl clerk was wrapping him and his men up in a large paper. "Very strange! Where have I heard those names before–Dick and Arnold? I wonder–I wonder—"

But just then the girl turned the box upside down to tie a knot in the string she was putting around it, and the Captain and his men had all they could do to keep in their places.

"Stand fast, every one of you!" said the Captain in a low voice to his tin men. "We are perhaps going on a long trip."

The boy paid over his dollar of pocket money, his father added another dollar, and then the box of toy Tin Soldiers was taken away.

Just what happened on their trip from the store of course the Captain and his men did not know. They could feel themselves being jiggled about, and at one time they were put on the seat of an automobile, though they did not know it. And finally they were set down with a jingle and a jangle, the guns of the men rattling against the tin legs of the soldiers, and the sword of the Captain tinkling in its scabbard.

"Now I'll have some fun with my Soldiers!" cried the boy, whose name was Arnold.

The paper was taken off, the box was opened, and once more the Bold Tin Soldier and his men saw the light of day. They looked about them curiously.

The Captain and his men saw that they were in a pleasant, sunny room. The box, which might have been called their "barracks," was on a table, and, bending over it, was the boy, Arnold.

"Forward–March!" called Arnold, and one by one he took the Tin Soldiers out of the box and set them in rows on the table, with the Captain at the head of his men. That is the proper place for a Captain, you know.

Of course if Arnold had not been there, and if no other human eyes had been looking at the Tin Soldiers, they could have marched out of the box by themselves. But, as it was, Arnold had to lift them out. He did not know, of course, that his toys, and all other toys, have the power of pretending they are alive at certain times.

As Arnold was standing his Soldiers in rows on the table, the door of the room opened and a little girl came in.

"Oh, Arnold! what did you get?" she asked. "Oh, aren't they nice!"

"These are my new Soldiers, Mirabell," said the boy. "Daddy took me to the store and I bought them with some of my pocket money. But Daddy gave me a dollar, too. Want to see my Soldiers fight?" asked Arnold, as he stood the Corporal and the Sergeant where they could help the Captain take charge of the men.

"Oh, no, Arnold! I don't want to see any soldiers fight! They might shoot me!" cried the little girl, pretending to shiver.

"Nope! They won't shoot anybody!" said Arnold. "They have only make-believe guns, and I'll only make-believe shoot 'em. I yell 'Bang! Bang!' and that's all the shooting there is. Now watch, Mirabell."

The boy divided the tin toys into two companies, just as the tin Captain himself had done with his men when he gave the fancy drill on the counter before the Calico Clown swung from the string and nearly caught fire. One of the companies was commanded by the Captain, while the Sergeant, who had red stripes on his sleeves, was in charge of the other.

"Now for the battle!" cried the boy. "Ready! Aim! Fire! Bang! Bang!" And he yelled so loudly that his sister Mirabell put her hands over her ears, just as, in the store, the Rag Doll had covered her ears.

"Mercy, don't shout so loud, Arnold!" cried Mirabell. "Oh, not so loud!"

"I have to. This is a big fight!" the boy answered. "Bang! Bang! Bang!"

Then he knocked some of the soldiers over, pretending they had fallen in battle, and he moved some forward across the table and some he moved back.

"One side is winning and the other side is losing," said the boy. "The losing side is running away. Bang! Bang! Bang!"

"This is too much for me!" said Mirabell. "There is too much bang-banging. I'm going to play with my Lamb on Wheels."

The Bold Tin Soldier Captain heard Mirabell say that, even above the noise made by Arnold.

"I Just Arrived," Answered the Bold Tin Soldier.

"I Just Arrived," Answered the Bold Tin Soldier.

"Ha! Now I know where I heard those names before!" thought the Captain. "The Sawdust Doll told us about these children when she came back to the store to visit that day. They live next door to Dick and Dorothy. Oh, I am in good company!"

Back and forth across the table the boy moved his two companies of Tin Soldiers. Sometimes he would make believe one side was winning the battle, and again he would let the other side seem to win.

The Captain and his men had little to say about it, for they could not move by themselves nor talk when Arnold was looking at them. And when he and his men were being moved back by the boy, and losing the pretend battle to the Sergeant and his men, the Captain sighed and said:

"Oh, if we could only do as we pleased! Then I'd show this boy how a real Tin Soldier can fight!"

But of course the Captain could not do that. He had to be content to let Arnold move him about. And the boy had fun with his company of Tin Soldiers.

He fought several battles with them, but at last, like all boys, he wanted to do something else. He was just wondering what he could do when the door opened, and Mirabell came in dragging behind her a rather large, woolly Lamb on Wheels.

"Come on out on the porch and play with me!" begged Mirabell of her brother. "It is nice out there, and you can bring your Soldiers with you."

"Yes, so I can," said Arnold. "I'll do it. Wait until I get the little wooden cannon that shoots paper bullets. I'll put that in the war."

"And I'll get my little Wooden Doll and pretend she is a Red Cross Nurse," said Mirabell.

Together the children ran from the room, leaving the Tin Soldiers on the table and the Lamb on Wheels on the floor.

"Well, of all things!" bleated the Lamb, when she saw the Bold Tin Soldier. "Just fancy seeing you again! When did you get here?"

"I just arrived," answered the Captain, for, there being no one in the room then, he and the Lamb could talk and move by themselves.

"I'm so glad you are here," went on the woolly pet "Tell me all that has happened at the store since I was taken away. Is the Candy Rabbit there yet? And the Monkey on a Stick and the Calico Clown? Are they all there?"

"Yes. But the Clown had a sad accident just before I came away," said the Captain.

"Dear me, how dreadful! Was he hurt?" eagerly asked the Lamb on Wheels, rolling over a little closer to the table on which stood the Tin Soldiers and their Captain. None of the Soldiers spoke while their Captain was talking, as that was not considered polite.

"No, the Clown wasn't exactly hurt," said the Captain, "but his trousers were scorched."

"Oh, his lovely red and yellow trousers!" bleated the Lamb. "How sad! Tell me about it, please!"

"Well, you see, the Clown was doing a few tricks to amuse us, and—"

"Hush, sir! Quiet if you please, sir!" exclaimed the Sergeant, saluting his Captain. "Some one is coming, sir! I hear them, sir!"

And just then the door opened and Mirabell and Arnold came running back into the room, the boy carrying a little wooden cannon and his sister with a Wooden Doll in her hand–the doll that was to be a Red Cross Nurse.

"Oh, Arnold! Look!" cried Mirabell.

"What's the matter?" asked her brother, as he began gathering up the Tin Soldiers.

"Why, look at my Lamb on Wheels!" went on Mirabell. "I left her over by the door, and now she has rolled over near the table."

"I guess the wind must have blown her," said Arnold.

"But the door wasn't open, nor the windows," went on Mirabell. "So how could the wind blow her? Oh, Arnold, once before my Lamb moved when I left her alone! Wouldn't it be wonderful if she could really be alive and move by herself?"

"Yes, it would," admitted Arnold. "But your Lamb can't move by herself any more than my Tin Soldiers can."

However, he little knew what went on after dark, when he and Mirabell were asleep in bed, did he?

"Now we'll go out on the porch and have some fun," said Arnold, putting his Soldiers back in their box.

It was a warm, sunny day, and soon the two children were having a good time out on the porch of their house. Arnold set his Soldiers in two rows, with the Captain at the head of one row and the Sergeant at the head of the other. Then the boy put some paper bullets in his toy, wooden cannon, and Mirabell wheeled her Lamb to a safe place.

Arnold was just going to shoot his cannon and pretend to have the tin guns of the Soldiers go bang-bang when, all at once, a shower of hard, dried beans fell on the porch. Some struck the Soldiers, some hit the Red Cross Doll, and some pattered on Mirabell and Arnold.

"Oh, some one is shooting bean bullets at us!" cried the little girl. "This is a bean battle! Are your Tin Soldiers shooting bean bullets, Arnold?"

CHAPTER V

THE CAPTAIN AND THE LAMB

For a few seconds Arnold did not know what to answer. One of the hard, dried beans had struck him on the nose, and, while it did not hurt very much, it made his eyes water and he could not see what was happening.

But the beans kept on falling about the porch, and one struck a Tin Soldier and knocked him over. This Soldier was a very small chap. He was, in fact, the drummer boy.

"But who is shooting the beans at us?" cried Mirabell, as she lay down on the porch behind her Lamb on Wheels.

"I don't know who is pegging beans at us," said Arnold, looking around and out toward the street. "It isn't my Soldiers, for their tin guns can only make believe shoot."

Just then some shouts were heard and more beans came rattling across the porch, some, once more, hitting the Lamb, Arnold, and the Tin Soldiers.

"Oh, look, Arnold!" suddenly called his sister. "I see who is doing it!"

"Who?" he asked.

"A lot of rough boys! Look! They, have bean-blowers!"

As she spoke more shouts sounded and more beans came flying swiftly over the porch.

"Shoot the Tin Soldiers! Shoot the Tin Soldiers!" cried the rough boys. There were three of them, and, as Mirabell had said, they had long tin bean, or putty, blowers. They were blowing the beans at the boy and his sister on the porch.

Rattle and bang went the hard dried beans, but the Bold Tin Soldier Captain and his men stood bravely up under the shower of bean bullets. The Red Cross Nurse Doll was brave, too, and did not run away, while the Lamb on Wheels stood on her wooden platform and never so much as blinked an eye as bean after bean struck her.

"Shoot the Tin Soldiers! Shoot the woolly Lamb!" cried the bad boys, as they, blew more beans.

"Here! You stop shooting beans at us!" cried Arnold. "Do you hear me? You stop it!"

"Ho! Ho! We won't stop for you! You can't make us!" shouted the boys, and they were going to blow more beans, but just then Patrick, the gardener next door, came along with some seeds he had been down to the store to buy.

"Patrick!" called Mirabell.

Patrick saw the bad boys blowing beans at Mirabell and Arnold, and, with a shout, the gardener chased the unpleasant lads away.

"Be off out of here and let my children alone!" cried Patrick, for he considered Dorothy and Dick and Arnold and Mirabell as his special "children," and was always watching to see that no harm came to them. And once Patrick had saved the Lamb on Wheels, as you may read in the book written specially about that toy.

"Did they hurt you, Mirabell or Arnold?" asked the gardener, as he came back from chasing the boys.

"No, thank you, not much," Arnold answered. "One bean struck me on the nose, but it didn't hurt–hardly any."

"And one bean knocked over one of your Soldiers, Arnold," said Mirabell.

"He's the drummer boy–I guess he isn't hurt any," returned the boy, and he set the Tin Drummer on his feet again.

"Well, well! You have a fine regiment of soldiers, there!" said Patrick. "A fine regiment. What are you going to do with 'em, Arnold?"

"We're going to have a make-believe battle, now that the boys with the beans have gone away," Arnold replied.

"And my Wooden Doll is going to be a Bed Cross Nurse," added Mirabell. "And if any of the Soldiers get hurt I'll give them a ride on the back of my Lamb."

"Oh, sure and you'll have dandy times!" laughed Patrick.

Then Arnold and Mirabell had fun playing on the porch with the Tin Soldiers, the wooden cannon, the Doll and the Lamb on Wheels. Back and forth Arnold marched his two companies of Soldiers, firing the make-believe guns in regular bang-bang style.

Sometimes he would pretend a Soldier was wounded, though, of course, none of them really was, and Mirabell would make the Red Cross Nurse Doll look after the injured. And when the battle was nearly over Arnold made believe that a dozen or more of his Tin Soldiers were hurt.

"Oh, my Doll nurse can't look after so many hurt soldiers!" objected the little girl. "There's too many!"

"Put 'em on the back of your Lamb and make believe it's an ambulance," said Arnold, and Mirabell did this.

So the two children continued to play together with Arnold's new soldier toys. And then, just as the last bang-bang gun was fired, Susan, the jolly, good-natured cook, called:

"Come, children! I have a little pie I baked especially for you two. It is just out of the oven! Come and get some while it is hot!"

And you may well believe that Mirabell and Arnold did not wait–they ran at once, leaving their toys on the porch.

"Well, now we have a chance to rest," said the Bold Tin Soldier Captain to his men. "Whew! that battle was surely as lively as the one we had in the store the other night."

"I should say so!" agreed the Sergeant. "The bayonet on my gun is bent."

"Well, that shows you have been to war," said the Captain. "And now we must thank the Red Cross Doll and the Lamb on Wheels for what they did for us during the make-believe fight."

"Oh, I didn't do much," cried the Wooden Doll, with a laugh. "None of you was really hurt, you know."

"That is true," agreed the Captain. "But if we had really been wounded you would have helped us, I am sure."

"Yes," admitted the Doll, "I surely would."

"And I was only too glad to have you ride on my back," said the Lamb on Wheels. "It is so good to meet you again, Captain," she went on. "Quite like old times. We have a few minutes now, while the children are away, getting their pie. Do tell me what happened to the Calico Clown."

"His trousers were burned," said the Captain. "And because Arnold bought me and my men I had to leave the store before I could see the new trousers the girl was going to make. But I'll tell you all about it," and the Bold Tin Soldier did.

"Did he ever tell the answer to that riddle of what it is that makes more noise than a pig under a gate?" asked the Lamb.

"No, he never did," said the Captain. "I meant to ask him, but I came away in a hurry, you see."

"Yes, we toys don't generally have much say as to what we shall or shall not do," bleated the Lamb. "I have been puzzling over that riddle myself."

"The next time I see the Calico Clown I will ask him the answer," declared the Captain. "There is no need of making such a secret about it. But, speaking of the store, it was lonesome there after you and the Sawdust Doll and the White Rocking Horse came away."

"Really? Did you miss me?" asked the Lamb.

"Indeed we did," declared the Captain. "And, in a way, I am glad I was bought and brought away. One reason is that now I may have some adventures, and another reason is that I have seen you again."

"It is very nice of you to say that," said the Lamb.

"Is there any chance of seeing the Sawdust Doll or the White Rocking Horse again?" asked the Captain.

"Yes, indeed! Every chance in the world," was the Lamb's answer. "Why, they only live next door. The Sawdust Doll belongs to a little girl named Dorothy, and the White Rocking Horse to a boy named Dick."

Then the Wooden Doll, who was a Red Cross Nurse, the Lamb on Wheels and the Bold Tin Soldier and his Tin Men talked together for some little time longer, while Arnold and Mirabell were in the kitchen eating the pie Susan had so kindly baked for them.

All of a sudden, as the Lamb was telling the Soldier some of her adventures, and how she had floated downstream on a raft, something fluttered down out of a tree near the porch, and the Lamb cried:

"Ouch!"

"What is the matter?" asked the Bold Tin Soldier. "Did a bee sting you?"

"No, that was a bird!" bleated the Lamb on Wheels. "And did you see what he did?"

"No! what?" asked the Soldier.

"Why, that bird flew right down out of a tree and grabbed a beak full of wool off my back," went on the Lamb. "Gracious, how he pulled!"

And while the Captain was getting ready to say something, down flew the bird again, and he plucked another beak full of loose, soft wool, pulling it from the Lamb's back.

"Ouch! Oh, how you pull! Please stop!" bleated the Lamb.

The Bold Tin Soldier drew his sword.

"Look here, Mr. Bird!" cried the Captain. "I do not want to hurt you, but I can not allow you to pull wool from the back of my friend, Miss Lamb. You must stop it, or I will drive you away with my shiny, tin sword, as I drove away the bad rat that wanted to nibble the ears of the Candy Rabbit! Stop it, Mr. Bird!"

"Tweet! Tweet! Tweet!" chirped the Bird. "Please let me pull some more wool from your back, Miss Lamb," and he fluttered in the air with his beak wide open, while the Bold Tin Soldier, with drawn sword, took a step forward.

What was going to happen?

CHAPTER VI

SAVING THE SAWDUST DOLL

The bird was just going to flutter down and pull some more wool from the back of the Lamb on Wheels, when the Bold Tin Soldier, waving his sword, happened to strike it on the iron wheels of the wooden platform on which Miss Lamb stood. The shiny sword made a clanking sound, and, hearing this, the bird, instead of fluttering to the Lamb's back, perched on the porch railing.

"Well, you'd better not come and pull any more wool from my friend, Miss Lamb!" said the Soldier Captain.

"Oh, please excuse me!" chirped the bird. "Oh, what a mistake I have made! Why, you are only a toy lamb, aren't you?" he asked the plaything.

"Of course I am a toy," answered the Lamb on Wheels. "But I can talk and move around when no human eyes watch me."

"That's just the trouble," said the bird. "I took you for a real lamb, and that is why I pulled some wool from your back. I wouldn't have done it for the world if I had known you were a toy! Please excuse me. I made a mistake."

"Do you mean to say," asked the Bold Tin Soldier, "that you could pull wool from the back of a real, live lamb?"

"Of course I could!" chirped the bird.

"What for?" asked the Wooden Doll.

"To line my nest with, of course," answered Mr. Bird. "You see I am helping my wife make a nest. She is going to lay eggs in it and hatch out baby birds. And we want the nest nice and soft for the little ones. So, when I saw the woolly Lamb here on the porch, I flew down to pick some soft stuff from her back. I never thought she was a toy."

"Don't the real lambs mind if you pull wool from their backs?" asked the Wooden Doll.

"Not at all," was the answer. "The real lambs, down in the green pasture by the brook, often have loose bits of wool on their backs. Other birds and I fly down, take off the loose pieces, and line our nests with them. Sometimes, when I can not get wool, I take the soft fluffy cotton from the milkweed plant, but I like lambs' fleece the best. It is so soft and warm for the little birds. But don't worry, Miss Lamb, I will not bother you again."

"I am sorry I can not let you have more of my wool," went on the Lamb on Wheels. "But, you see, not being real, my wool is glued fast to my back, and

26

every time you take some off it pulls. And I can't grow any more like a real lamb."

"Yes, I know," chirped the bird. "Well, now I will fly to the green meadow and get some wool from a real lamb. Please forgive me, friends, for making trouble."

"Oh, that's all right," said the Bold Tin Soldier, putting away his shiny sword.

So, when the bird had flown away, the three toys were happy together again–the Bold Tin Soldier Captain, the Lamb on Wheels, and the Wooden Doll. Then the children came back to have more fun, and the toys had to be very still and quiet, moving about only as Arnold or Mirabell moved them.

When supper time came Arnold put his Tin Soldiers back in their box, and set them away on a shelf in the dark closet. He also put his wooden cannon there, while Mirabell put her Doll and other toys on the floor of the closet, as she could not quite reach up to the shelf.

"Do you think you are going to like it here, Captain?" asked one of the Tin Soldiers, when the closet door was shut and the toys could do as they pleased, since no eyes could see them.

"Yes, I think this will be a nice place," was the answer. "Arnold is going to be kind to us, I can see that."

"Yes, sir, he is a fine boy."

"I shouldn't think you would like being made to fight so often," said the Wooden Doll. "Dear me, you seem to do nothing but go into battle and shoot your guns or draw your swords!"

"That is a soldier's life," said the Captain. "That is what we were made for, to fight and protect the weak. If ever you need our help, just call on us, Miss Doll."

The next morning Arnold opened the closet and took out his box of Tin Soldiers where they stood in their places straight and stiff, with their Captain at their head.

"What are you going to do, Arnold?" asked Mirabell.

"I'm going over to Dick's house to have some fun," he answered. "I will let him play with my Soldiers, and he will let me ride on his White Rocking Horse."

"Oh, then I'm going over and take my Lamb!" exclaimed Mirabell. "I'll let Dorothy play with her, and maybe she'll let me take her Sawdust Doll."

"Come on. We'll have lots of fun," said Arnold.

So the children, with their toys, went next door to the house where Dick and Dorothy lived. Mirabell and Arnold found their friends out on the lawn, and Dick had his Rocking Horse while Dorothy was playing with her Sawdust Doll.

"Oh, now we will have some dandy fun!" cried Dick. "Let me see your new Tin Soldiers, Arnold."

The grass was nice and smooth, and soon the Bold Tin Captain and his men were set up in rows, just as if they were on parade. Dick took half the Tin Soldiers and Arnold the other half, and then the little boys pretended to have a battle, only, of course, no one was hurt.

"May I ride your Rocking Horse?" asked Arnold, presently.

"Of course," answered Dick. "You take a nice, long ride, while I play with your Soldiers."

And while this was going on Mirabell and Dorothy played with the Sawdust Doll and the Lamb on Wheels. And how the toys did wish they were alone, so they could talk to one another! Of course the Sawdust Doll and the Rocking Horse, living in the same house, saw each other very often, and at night they could talk and play together. But it had been some time since either of them had seen the Bold Tin Soldier and his men, and the Doll and Horse were very anxious to hear the news from the store.

"Oh, my dear!" whispered the Lamb on Wheels to the Sawdust Doll, when they had a chance to talk together alone for a moment, which was when Dorothy and Mirabell went into the house to get some crackers for a play party, "you have no idea what an exciting story the Bold Tin Soldier has to tell you!"

"What about?" asked the Sawdust Doll.

"About how he saved the Calico Clown," was the answer. "He'll tell you about it when he has the chance."

"I shall be glad to hear it," said the Sawdust Doll. "But I hope nothing serious happened to the Clown."

"No. But it might have," answered the Lamb. "Hush! Here come the children back. We may not talk any longer."

But a little later on there was a chance for all four of the toys to talk among themselves. And there was quite an adventure, too, for the Bold Tin Soldier and the Sawdust Doll.

After they had played for some time, Dorothy and Mirabell and Dick and Arnold saw Patrick, the gardener, get out the hose.

"Oh, may we sprinkle a little?" cried Dick.

"Yes, please let us squirt some water on the flowers," begged Dorothy.

"If you'll be very careful not to get wet you may," said Patrick.

Over the lawn ran the four children, leaving their toys on the grass. And, seeing this, the Bold Tin Soldier said:

"Ah, now we have a chance to do as we please!"

"Then you must please tell me how you saved the Calico Clown," begged the Sawdust Doll.

"Shiver my sword!" cried the Soldier, laughing, "have you heard that story, also? It was nothing–just a little happening. We soldiers must do our duty, you know."

"Yes, but tell me about it," begged the Doll, and the Captain did.

"My, how brave you are!" said the Sawdust Doll, when he had finished. "And now tell me about the Candy Rabbit, the Monkey on a Stick, the Elephant on Roller Skates, and all the others."

"Yes, do tell her," urged the Lamb.

"Yes, I want to hear about the Elephant," said the White Rocking Horse. "He tried to race with me once. Ha! Ha! That was funny!"

So the Bold Tin Soldier told of the happenings in the toy department of the store, and the toys were having a good time among themselves when, all of a sudden, into the yard ran a big dog. He was much larger than Carlo, the poodle dog that had once carried off the Sawdust Doll in his mouth.

With a wiff-wuffing bark this dog ran right among the toys who were talking together.

"Oh dear me!" cried the Sawdust Doll.

"Ha! what is the matter with you?" asked the dog, who was neither very good nor very polite. "What are you 'oh dearing' about? I guess I'll just take you home to let my puppies play with you!"

He sprang towards the Sawdust Doll and was just going to pick her up in his mouth, when the Bold Tin Soldier drew his sword.

"Keep away from my friend, the Sawdust Doll!" cried the Captain.

"Who says so?" barked the big dog.

"I do!" answered the Tin Soldier. "I will save the Sawdust Doll from being carried away!"

CHAPTER VII

A SAD ACCIDENT

If the big dog had not been so gruff and impolite, and if he had known how truly brave the Bold Tin Soldier was, the barking chap never would have tried to do what he said he was going to do–carry away the Sawdust Doll.

"Yes, I am going to take the Sawdust Doll home to my kennel, so my little puppies will have something to gnaw and to play with," went on the big dog.

"Oh, just fancy!" exclaimed the poor Doll. "Oh, I don't want to be gnawed and played with by any puppies! They may bite holes in me, and all my sawdust will run out I Oh dear!"

"Don't be afraid," replied the Bold Tin Soldier. "This dog shall not take you away."

"Bow wow! You just watch me!" barked the bad dog. He ran at the Sawdust Doll with wide-open mouth, but before he could pick her up to carry her away the Bold Tin Soldier thrust his sword at the dog and pricked him on the paw.

"Ouch! Oh, dear! I must have run a thorn into my foot!" howled the dog.

"No, it was not a thorn. It was my sword that pricked you," said the Bold Tin Soldier. "I only stuck you a little bit this first time, but if you keep on teasing my friend, Miss Sawdust Doll, I shall have to do something worse. You had better run away!"

"Yes, I think I had," howled the dog. "I didn't know your sword was so sharp. Ouch, my paw hurts!"

"Well, I am sorry I had to hurt you," said the Captain. "But if you had behaved yourself it would not have happened."

"I'll put a grass poultice on it," said the Sawdust Doll. "I know something about nursing, for once in a while Dorothy pretends I am in a hospital. I'll bind some grass on your foot, Mr. Dog, if you will promise to let me alone."

"Yes, I'll do that," was the barking answer. "And I am sorry I was so unkind to you. Please forgive me!"

The Sawdust Doll said she would. Then the Bold Tin Soldier, with the same sword that had pricked the dog, cut some grass, and it was bound on the dog's paw. The sword prick was not a very deep one, and would soon heal. Then, limping on three legs, the dog ran away, and the toys were left to themselves once more.

By this time Patrick had let the children do all the hose sprinkling he thought was good for them, so back came running Dick and Dorothy, Arnold and Mirabell, to play with their toys again.

"What shall we play now?" asked Dick of Arnold. "Shall we have another battle with the Tin Soldiers?"

"Let's go to the garage and play we're going on an automobile trip," said Arnold. "We have had enough battles today."

So the Captain and his men were put back in their box and the cover was closed down.

"Oh, dear!" thought the Lamb on Wheels. "Now if anything happens, such as a big dog coming again, the Captain can not save us. He can not get out of the box."

But the Lamb need not have worried, for she was taken into the house by Mirabell, and so was the Sawdust Doll and the Rocking Horse. The little girls went down the street to play with a friend named Madeline, leaving their own toys in Dorothy's house, while Dick and Arnold went out to the garage, and from there over to Arnold's house.

But though no big dog came into the home of Dick and Dorothy to carry away the Sawdust Doll, something else happened, almost as bad, at least for the Bold Tin Soldier.

He and his men had been put in their box, and the box was put on a table in the playroom, together with the Lamb on Wheels, the Sawdust Doll and the White Rocking Horse. When Arnold and Mirabell went home they would take the Soldiers and the Lamb with them.

But before this came about something happened. A lady came to call on Dorothy's mother, bringing with her a little boy named Tad. Now Tad was not a bad little boy, but he was always looking for something to play with and he was not careful.

When Tad reached the home of Dick and Dorothy and found neither of the children was in, and when he saw his mother and Dorothy's mother talking together, Tad wandered about by himself to find something with which he could have fun. And the first thing he saw was the box of Tin Soldiers.

"Oh, now I can have some fun!" cried Tad.

He opened the box and took out the Bold Tin Captain. Then he took out the other Soldiers, the Sergeant, the Corporal and all the men.

"Ha! Now I can have a battle!" cried Tad, and he threw all the Soldiers in a heap on the floor.

"Oh, my, this little fellow is a dreadful chap!" thought the Captain. "If he isn't careful he will break some of us."

"I'm glad we don't belong to him!" thought the Sergeant.

Still the Soldiers could do nothing, nor could they say anything, as Tad was there looking at them with his big, blue eyes. And Tad did more than look. He handled the Tin Soldiers very roughly.

The carpet was so soft that when they were thrown out of their box they were not hurt, but as Tad grew rougher and rougher as he handled the Captain and his men, the Bold Tin Soldier began to be very much worried.

"Stand up there!" cried Tad, and he jabbed the Soldiers, one after the other, down very hard on the carpet. Now the carpet, being soft and thick, was not a very good place for the Soldiers to stand on. They fell over very easily, and, seeing this, Tad cried:

"Stand up there!"

And when the Soldiers kept falling over–since they dared not spread their legs and act as if they were alive when any human eyes were watching them–Tad cried impatiently:

"Oh, you're no good! I'm not going to play with you! I'm going to have some other fun!"

With a sweep of his hand he sent the Soldiers in a heap together. Some fell one way and some another, and the Captain bounced out to the middle of the floor where Tad let him lay.

"I guess I'll ride on the Rocking Horse!" cried this not-very-good little boy.

"Oh, dear me! now I am in for a time," thought the White Horse. "This little lad is as rough as the one who used to dig his heels into my sides when he jumped on my back in the store. Oh, there he comes!"

And, surely enough, Tad ran across the room and climbed up on the back of the White Rocking Horse. If the Horse could have had his way he would have turned and galloped out of the room. But he could not do this, and so he just had to stand there and take what came.

"Gid-dap, there! Gid-dap!" cried Tad, banging his heels against the sides of the White Rocking Horse.

Now, as I have told you, when the Horse was made to rock back and forth he traveled along, just as sometimes a rocking chair moves across the room. And the faster Tad made the horse sway to and fro, the more the wooden toy moved along.

"Oh, I'm really having a ride!" cried Tad. "This is fun! Gid-dap, White Rocking Horse!"

Over the room on the soft carpet rocked the Horse, straight toward the Bold Tin Soldier who was lying in the middle of the room. And in a few moments, unless Tad stopped rocking the Horse, he would run over his friend, the Captain.

"Gid-dap! Gid-dap!" shouted Tad.

The Horse saw what was going to happen, and so did the Captain.

"Oh, if I can only get out of the way!" thought the Bold Tin Soldier.

"Oh, if only I do not have to rock on my bold friend!" thought the White Horse.

"Gid-dap! Gid-dap!" cried Tad again, and he made the Horse go faster and faster.

Nearer and nearer the rockers went to the Bold Tin Soldier. He wanted to shout aloud, but that was against the rules. And the Horse wanted to stop and turn about, and that, also, was against the rules, as long as Tad was there. As for the boy himself, I don't really believe he would have done it if he had seen what was going to happen.

But he was so excited at being on the back of the Horse that he did not look down at the floor where the Bold Tin Soldier lay. And a moment later the Horse rocked, with a crunching sound, right over his friend!

CHAPTER VIII

A BUNCH OF SWEETNESS

The Bold Tin Soldier wanted to shout aloud and yell when he felt the rockers of the White Rocking Horse going over him. But he was a truly brave chap, and he knew it would never do to let that careless boy Tad know a Tin Soldier could pretend to be alive.

"I must not say a word!" thought the Soldier to himself.

And you can just imagine how the White Rocking Horse felt when he was made to run over his dear friend from the toy store!

"Oh, dear me," said the White Rocking Horse to himself, when he heard the crunching sound, "something dreadful has happened! But it was not my fault! It was that boy's!"

For you know, as well as I do, that if the White Rocking Horse had had his way he would have turned out, and not have gone over his friend, the Captain.

But Tad did not stop rocking, even when he heard the crunching sound. He swayed backward and forward in the saddle and cried:

"Gid-dap! Go faster!"

And he made the White Rocking Horse keep on. I don't know what else would have happened. Maybe that careless boy would have rocked over the rest of the Tin Soldiers for all I know, only he happened to see the Lamb on Wheels.

"I'll pull her around. That will be fun," said Tad, springing off the back of the horse.

As the boy leaped from the back of the White Rocking Horse he turned that wooden chap half around so the animal could look at the Bold Tin Soldier lying on the carpet.

"Oh, my poor friend!" thought the White Rocking Horse, not daring to speak out loud, of course. "I hope you are not killed."

And I am glad to say that the Tin Soldier Captain was not. He was not even hurt, for the rocker of the horse had gone over his sword, instead of over one of the legs or arms of the toy chap. The Soldier's sword had been run over and broken off, scabbard and all. And the scabbard, or case in which the sword was kept, and the sword itself were lying on the floor, not far from the Captain.

"Dear me, what a sad accident!" thought the White Rocking Horse.

And the Bold Tin Soldier was thinking to himself:

"Well, it is lucky I am not hurt, but it is dreadful to have my sword broken off. My men may think I am no longer their captain, and they may not obey me. Oh, dear, I am no good any more!"

"I wonder if the rough boy will break me?" thought the Lamb on Wheels, as Tad dragged her around the room.

But Tad seemed more gentle with the Lamb, or else perhaps he was tired of playing with the toys. For all he did was to drag the woolly plaything around the room a few times, and then he let go the string.

"I'm hungry!" said Tad out loud. "I'm going to get my mother to ask Dorothy's mother to give me something to eat!"

Out of the room ran the boy, and all the toys breathed easier when they saw him go.

"My poor, dear friend!" exclaimed the Rocking Horse, as he slowly made his way over to where the Tin Soldier lay on the carpet. "I hope you will forgive me!"

"It was not your fault at all!" said the Soldier. "It could not be helped. It is the fortune of war, as we men of the army say. My sword is broken, that is true, but it is much better to bear that than to put up with a broken arm or leg. Perhaps I can be mended."

He picked up the sword which had been broken off from his tin side where it had been soldered, or fastened. He tried to make it stick on, but it was of no use.

"Never mind, Captain," said the Corporal from the floor where he lay in a heap with the other soldiers, "we think just as much of you as before. You are still our commander, sword or no sword!"

"I am glad to have you say that," returned the Bold Tin Soldier. "Dear me, what a day it has been!"

He was still holding the broken sword in his hand when the door opened again and some one came rushing in. The Soldier had to drop back on the carpet, letting his broken sword fall where it would, and neither the Horse nor the other toys could speak again for a time.

And then a voice said:

"Oh, look at my nice Soldiers on the floor!"

"And the Captain's sword is broken!" said another voice. "Oh, who do you suppose did it?"

It was Dick and Arnold who had come into the room.

"What is the matter?" asked Dick's mother, coming up to the playroom just then. "Has anything happened?"

"It Was Not Your Fault," Said the Soldier.

"It Was Not Your Fault," Said the Soldier.

Then the boys showed the sword broken from the side of the brave Captain.

"Tad must have done that!" said Dick's mother. "He was up here while his mother and I were talking downstairs. Oh, I am so sorry! But I will have your Soldier mended, Arnold."

"Do you think you can?" he asked.

"Oh, yes," was the answer. "Patrick, our gardener, is very good at soldering things. Once he soldered a hole in my dishpan. I will get him to fasten on the sword which is broken from your Tin Captain."

Patrick was called in. The gardener, who did many things around the big house besides watering the lawn and looking after the flowers, took the Bold Tin Soldier and the broken sword up in his hands.

"Can he be mended?" asked Dick's mother.

"Oh, yes, I think so," answered Patrick.

"And may we watch you mend him?" asked Arnold.

"May we, Patrick?" echoed Dick.

"Yes," answered the good-natured gardener. "Come along!"

Back to the garage he went where he had been mending something that was broken on the automobile, taking the Tin Soldier with him and followed by the two boys. Patrick heated a soldering iron in a little furnace in which burned glowing charcoal. Then Patrick took some shining metal that looked like silver, but which was really soft lead.

Solder melts easily, and when some is placed on two pieces of broken tin and heated, it holds together the two pieces of tin just as glue holds together pieces of cardboard or paper.

In a little while the Bold Tin Soldier was mended, and there he stood, straight and stiff, with his sword at his side as before. And where the sword had been soldered on a tiny spot of bright lead showed.

"I can paint that spot over for you tomorrow, when I have some red paint," said Patrick to Arnold.

"Oh, I know what I can do I" cried Arnold, looking at the shiny spot of lead. "I can pretend that is a medal my Captain got in the battle when his sword was broken."

"Yes, you can do that," agreed Dick.

So the toy was mended again, and was almost as good as before, and very glad the Captain was.

"For no matter what your men may say," he thought to himself, "a Captain without a sword is like an elephant without a trunk–he doesn't look himself."

Thanking Patrick very much for what he had done in mending the toy, Arnold went home, taking his set of Soldiers with him. A little later his sister, Mirabell, followed, bringing with her the Lamb on Wheels. And when the two toys were left alone, the children having gone to supper, they talked together–did the Soldier and the Lamb.

"You are certainly having plenty of adventures," said the Lamb, in her bleating voice.

"Yes. And for a time, when I saw the White Rocking Horse bearing down on me, I thought all my adventures were over," replied the Bold Tin Soldier.

"I hope that careless boy never comes around where we are again," said the Lamb, and the Soldier hoped the same thing.

And now I must tell you another adventure that happened to the Bold Tin Soldier. It was about a week after the White Rocking Horse had run over him, and he was getting used to the shiny "medal," as Arnold called it, that one day when the boy was having a make-believe battle with his Tin Soldiers Mirabell called from the kitchen:

"Oh, Arnold, come on down! Susan has baked some lovely cookies!"

"I'm coming!" cried Arnold, and, as he happened to have the Bold Tin Soldier in his hand just then, he took the Captain along when he ran down to the kitchen.

"Where are the cookies?" asked Arnold, who was feeling hungry.

"Right here on the table," replied Susan. "Put your Soldier down, Arnold, and sit up and eat."

Now, as it happened, there was an open barrel of sugar in the kitchen. The cook had taken some sugar out to use in making the cookies, and had forgotten to put the cover back on. And Arnold, being in a hurry, put his Captain down on a little shelf just over this barrel.

How it happened no one seemed to know, but perhaps in eating his cookie Arnold struck the Captain with his elbow. Anyhow, down into the sugar barrel fell the Bold Tin Soldier.

"Oh my! Now I am a bunch of sweetness!" thought the Captain, as he felt the grains of sugar rolling all over him. "Oh this is certainly a strange adventure! What a sweet time I shall have!"

CHAPTER IX

BACK TO THE STORE

The moment he had fallen into the barrel of sugar the Bold Tin Soldier scrambled to his feet and wiggled around until he got his head sticking up above the pile of sweet, white grains.

"If I don't do that, I may drown," he thought. "It would be strange to drown in a barrel of sugar! I don't want to do that!"

So he wiggled around until he could stand upright, buried to his neck in the sugar, but with his head out so he could look around with his painted tin eyes and breathe through his tin nose. Otherwise he would have smothered.

The barrel was not full of sugar. In fact, it was only about a foot deep on the bottom, but that was enough to more than cover the Bold Tin Soldier from sight if it should get over his head. And, being low down in the barrel as he was, the sides of it hid him from the sight of Arnold and the cook.

"These are good cookies, Susan," said Arnold, as he ate the last crumbs of the dainty the cook had given him.

"I'm glad you like them," she said. "Would you care for another?"

"Thank you, yes," the boy answered. And just as Susan was giving him one, and also passing another to Mirabell, Dick, the boy from next door, cried:

"Come on out into the yard, Arnold. I have a new little kitten!"

"Oh, I want to see it!" shouted Mirabell.

"So do I," added Arnold. "And please, Susan, may I have a cookie for Dick?"

"Yes," answered the good-natured cook.

So out to the yard rushed the children, Arnold forgetting all about his Tin Captain. And as Susan was very busy, she gave no thought to the Bold Tin Soldier. In fact, if she had thought of him at all, she would have imagined that Arnold had taken his toy with him.

So while the children were out playing with Dick's new kitten, and while the cook worked in the kitchen, the Captain stayed in the barrel of sugar.

"Well, this is certainly an adventure," thought the Captain, "and, though it is a sweet one, I can not say I altogether like it. I wonder how I can get out of here? I must get back to my men, or they will think I have deserted them. That would never do for a soldier!"

He looked up toward the open top of the barrel. It seemed far above his head, but he thought if he could cut little steps in the wooden sides of the barrel with his shiny tin sword he might be able to climb out.

"But of course I'll have to wait until night, when everything is still and quiet," thought the Captain to himself. "It would never do for me to be seen cutting my way up out of a barrel of sugar. That would give away the great secret of Toy-land-that we can move of ourselves. Yes, I must wait until after dark."

So, buried up to his neck in sugar as he was, the Bold Tin Soldier stood in the sweetness like a sentinel on guard. He was doing his duty in the barrel, as he had done it when he cut down the Calico Clown and saved that chap from burning at the gas jet.

"I should like to see the Clown now," thought the Captain. "It is lonesome here. But if the Calico Clown saw me he would make up some joke or riddle about me, very likely."

Then all of a sudden there was a loud, banging noise and it became very dark.

"Hello! what's that?" said the Bold Tin Soldier to himself. "It's as dark as night in here now, but I never knew evening to come as suddenly as that."

Truly it was as dark as night in the sugar barrel now, but it was not because night had come. It was because the cook had put the cover on the barrel, for she had finished her baking for the day.

But the Captain thought it was night, and since he was sure no one could see him now he drew his sword from the scabbard, or case, and started to get ready to cut little steps in the sides of the barrel to make a place where he might climb to the top.

While this was going on Arnold and Mirabell were out looking at Dick's pet kitten. Truly it was a little fluffy one, and so soft that the children loved to pet it. But after a while Arnold thought of his Bold Tin Soldier.

"Oh, I left the Captain on the shelf in the kitchen," said the little boy. "I must go get him and put him with the others."

Back to the kitchen he ran.

"What is it now?" asked Susan, who was getting ready to go out, for it was her afternoon off. "Do you want more cookies, Arnold?"

"No, thank you. I want my Tin Captain," he answered. "I left him here."

"Oh, you mean your Soldier," said the cook. "I haven't seen him. I don't believe you left him here."

"Oh, yes I did!" declared Arnold.

But the Bold Tin Soldier was not in sight, of course, being down in the barrel of sugar, as we know. And though Arnold and the cook looked for him they could not find him.

"Oh dear!" sighed Arnold, when he could not find the commander of his tin army, "where is he?"

"You must have taken him out into the yard and forgotten about it," said the cook.

"No I didn't," said the little boy.

"Then it is among your other playthings," the cook went on. "You had better look."

So Arnold looked, and his mother and Mirabell and Dick helped him, but the Bold Tin Soldier could not be found. He was not with the others in their box, and, look as he did, Arnold could not find his toy anywhere.

"I'll never get another like him," sighed the little boy. "He was so nice, with his shiny medal-button!"

"And he was such a good Captain!" added Dick.

And all this while the Bold Tin Soldier was in the dark barrel of sugar and was getting ready to climb up and out if he could!

No one was in the kitchen now. The cook had gone away and it was not yet time for supper. So, all unseen as he was in the barrel, the Tin Soldier could do as he pleased.

With his tin sword he began cutting little niches, or steps, in the wooden sides of the barrel. But as the wood was quite hard, and as the tin sword was not very sharp, it was not very easy work for the Captain.

As the afternoon passed, the other Soldiers in their box on a shelf in the playroom closet began to wonder what had become of their Captain.

"Some of us ought to go in search of him," said the Sergeant.

"Yes, but we can't go until after dark, when no one will see us moving about," answered the Corporal. "That's the worst of being a toy–we can not do as we please."

"I hope the Captain has not deserted us," said a private soldier.

"Deserted! I should say not!" cried the Sergeant. "Our Captain would never desert!"

Evening came. The cook came back and began to get supper. And by this time the Captain, in the sugar barrel, had cut several little niches in the sides of the barrel. He was working away so hard that he never heard the cook come into the kitchen and start to get supper.

Then, all of a sudden, the cook, as she went to the pantry to get some flour, stopped near the barrel of sugar. She heard a queer little sound coming from it.

"I declare!" exclaimed the cook, "a mouse is trying to gnaw into the sugar barrel! The idea!"

The sound the cook heard was the Captain's tin sword as he cut steps in the side of the barrel, so he might climb up. But this noise sounded exactly like the gnawing of a mouse.

"Get away from there!" cried the cook, and she quickly lifted the cover off the sugar barrel, letting in a flood of light, for it was now night and the electric lights were glowing. "Get out!" cried the cook, thinking to scare away the mouse, as she thought it was.

Now of course as soon as the sugar barrel was opened, and the moment the cook looked in, the Captain had to stop work. Back into its scabbard went his sword, and he settled down among the grains of sugar again. He was now being looked at by human eyes, and it was against the toy rule for him to move.

"Well I do declare!" cried the cook, as she glanced at the Bold Tin Soldier lying in the sugar. "Here is Arnold's Captain he has been looking for. He is in the kitchen, after all, but how did he get in this barrel? And where is the mouse that was gnawing?"

Of course there was no mouse–it was the Captain's sword making the noise. But the cook did not know that.

She leaned down and picked the Captain up in her fingers. So he got out of the sugar barrel after all, you see, without having to cut a ladder in the wood.

"Arnold! Arnold!" called Susan up the back stairs. "I have found your Tin Captain!"

"Where was he?" asked the little boy, who was playing with the other soldiers, and wishing he had their commander.

"He was in the barrel of sugar," was the answer. "You must have dropped him in when you were eating cookies this afternoon."

"Maybe I did!" said the boy. "Oh, I am so glad to get you back!" he went on, as he carried the Captain upstairs. "Thank you, Susan!"

Then the Bold Tin Soldier was placed at the head of his men on the table, and they were together once more.

"What happened to you? Why were you away from us so long?" whispered the Sergeant to the Captain, when Arnold went out of the room a moment.

"I was in a barrel of sugar," was the answer. "I'll tell you about it later."

And that night, when all was still and quiet in the house, the Captain told his story.

"That was a wonderful adventure!" said the Corporal.

"Yes," agreed the Captain, "it was. I wish the toys back at the store could hear it. I rather think it would surprise the Calico Clown."

Arnold was playing with his tin toys one day when his mother called to him.

"Arnold, get on your overcoat. I am going to take you and Mirabell down to the toy store. I want to get a little Easter present for your cousin Madeline."

"Oh, what fun!" cried Arnold, and before he thought what he was doing he thrust the Tin Captain into his coat pocket and took him with him when he went with his mother and sister to the store; that's what Arnold did.

"Dear me! what is going to happen now?" thought the Bold Tin Soldier, as he found himself in Arnold's pocket on his way back to the store.

CHAPTER X

THE SOLDIER AND THE RABBIT

Arnold and Mirabell rode up in the store elevator with their mother to the floor where the toys were displayed.

"What did you say you wanted to get for Madeline?" asked Mirabell, as she walked along looking at the pretty things on the counters and shelves.

"A little Easter present," was the answer. "Perhaps I can find some pretty little bunny, or a novelty of some sort, that Madeline would like. You children may help me pick it out."

"I'm going to see if there are any more Tin Soldiers like mine," said Arnold.

The children and their mother came near the toy counter. On it were many playthings that boys and girls like. The Calico Clown was there, the Monkey on a Stick, a Jumping Jack, and others.

"Oh, I wish I had that Jumping Jack!" exclaimed Arnold.

"But you have plenty of toys," said his mother.

"Yes, I know," he answered. "But I wish–I er–wish–I er–a-ker-choo!" suddenly sneezed Arnold, and as he felt his nose tickling he took his handkerchief from his pocket with a jerk.

And with the handkerchief out came the Bold Tin Soldier which the boy had stuffed into his pocket when he hurried downstairs as his mother called him to go shopping with her and Mirabell.

Out popped the Bold Tin Soldier, and he bounced right over on to the toy counter, just the very same place where he had lived before he came to Arnold's house.

"Oh. look!" cried Mirabell. "How funny! I didn't know you had brought your Tin Soldier Captain with you, Arnold."

"I didn't know it myself! I guess I must have stuffed him into my pocket and forgotten about him," the little boy said. "But I am not going to leave him here. I like him too much."

As it happened, the Bold Tin Soldier, when he was pulled out with the handkerchief, landed on the toy counter right side up, standing on his feet. And, as it also happened, he landed near the Candy Rabbit.

"I didn't know, my dear, that you were going to bring any of your toys with you," said Arnold's mother, with a smile.

"I didn't know it either!" he answered, with a laugh. He reached out his hand to pick up his Soldier and put him back in his pocket when, down at the other end of the toy counter, one of the clerks suddenly began spinning a humming top, which showed different colors and played a little tune as it whirled around.

"Oh, I want to see that!" cried Arnold.

"So do I!" echoed Mirabell.

"Perhaps that would be an Easter toy for Madeline," thought Mother.

So all three of them moved down toward the end of the toy counter, Arnold, for the moment, forgetting about his Tin Captain, who was thus left standing among his old friends with no one to watch him or them.

"Oh, how glad we are to see you here again!" exclaimed the Calico Clown. "We have only a moment before the folks come back, but tell us all about your adventures."

Bold Tin Soldier Compliments Calico Clown.

Bold Tin Soldier Compliments Calico Clown.

"Oh, it would take too long," said the Bold Tin Soldier. "I have had some remarkable ones, but falling into a sugar barrel was the queerest. But what a fine pair of trousers you have, Clown," he said.

The funny chap looked pleased at this.

"Yes, these are the new ones the girl made for me after I scorched mine climbing the string too near the gas–the time you saved me, you know," replied the Clown.

"My! you look gay enough for a circus," said the Soldier.

"I'd like to join one," the Clown went on. "But I don't suppose there is any chance. I've been on this toy counter so long I'm beginning to believe I shall always live here. But you–you have been out to see the world! You have had adventures!"

"Yes, I suppose you may say I have," admitted the Bold Tin Soldier. "But though my men and I have a fine home with Arnold, still I get lonesome for you toys once in a while. I have met the Sawdust Doll, the White Rocking Horse, and the Lamb on Wheels. Now I am glad to meet you all once more. And how is my friend the Candy Rabbit?" the Captain asked, as he saw the long-eared chap standing near him.

"I am quite well, thank you," the Rabbit answered. "It will soon be Easter, and then perhaps my adventures will begin."

"It certainly is good to see you again," said the Monkey on a Stick to the Captain. "I have been wishing I could get away from here for a time, to have some adventures, but, so far, I haven't had a chance."

"Your time will come," said the Captain. "You are such a lively chap that I should think you would have many things happen to you."

"Yes, I'm not slow, whatever else you may say about me," chattered the Monkey, and, with that, he turned a somersault on his stick, but of course none of the people in the store saw him, for that was not allowed, you know.

"Hush! The people are coming back!" suddenly called the Candy Rabbit, and, surely enough, Mirabell, Arnold and their mother came back after having seen the buzzing top.

"I think that would not be just the right kind of an Easter present I want for Madeline," said Mirabell's mother. "I'll look here, among the toys."

"Why don't you get her a Candy Rabbit?" asked Mirabell.

"I believe I will," said Mother. She picked the Candy Rabbit up and looked at him. He was a fine fellow, colored just like a real rabbit, and with pink eyes and a pink nose.

"Oh, now my adventures will soon begin," thought the Candy Rabbit.

"I think this will do very nicely for Madeline," said the mother of the two children. "I will come at Easter for it," she went on to the clerk. "Come, children."

And when Arnold had picked up his Bold Tin Soldier and put him back in his pocket, the children and their mother left the store.

The Captain wished he might have had another chance to speak to his toy friends, but it was not to be just then.

"I wonder if I shall see the Candy Rabbit again," he thought as he made himself comfortable in Arnold's warm pocket.

In a little while the children were back home again after the shopping trip.

"I am going to play with my Lamb on Wheels," said Mirabell. "I am going to take her over to Dorothy's house to see the Sawdust Doll."

"And I'll take my Soldiers over and have some fun with Dick and his White Rocking Horse," said Arnold.

And when the four toys in Dick's house had a chance to talk among themselves, as the children were out of the room for a while, the Captain said:

"Oh, I have such news for you!"

"What is it?" asked the Sawdust Doll.

"I think the Candy Rabbit is going to be sent to a little girl named Madeline for an Easter present," said the Captain.

"Why, that girl-Madeline-lives right across the street!" exclaimed the White Rocking Horse. "She is Mirabell's cousin, and she knows Dorothy."

"Oh, then maybe we shall see the Candy Rabbit again," said the Bold Tin Soldier. "I am glad of that!"

And as for what happened next-well, if you wish to know you may find out by reading the next book of this series, which will be called "The Story of a Candy Rabbit." In it you will again meet the Bold Tin Soldier and all his friends.

THE END